MIRROR WORLD

MADNESS

-AYESHA MUNNI

Every story is possible until it is not

1

"It's just a theory!" shouted professor MCDougal with a crabby voice. On hearing those words, her grey eyes filled with despair, her usually pale face turned red. The fire burned brightly in the background and the soft radiance of the incandescent lights in the lilies of silver caught the bubbles that flashed and passed in the glasses of all the members sitting in the conference hall. Everyone were quietly waiting for her reply that, whether she accepts the fact of Dougal or she had anything else to say. The dejected REGAL lifted her voice " Even if it is just a theory , what's wrong in trying to prove it ?" in a fiery way, as her presented model representing PARALLEL UNIVERSE seemed a senseless topic to MCDougal, the professor of astrophysics, who was recently got hype due to his contribution in cosmological crafts.

But it seemed a logical thought to the chairman of the conference named ASTRO-ATOMIC CONFERENCE which was held by NASA as a part of up skilling the students of post matriculation and to obtain the students with impressive ideas in Stanford university of USA.

Finally the conference ended after listening to the ideas of others too. Everyone left the conference hall. While Regal was leaving, the chairman called her and apprised her saying "Your thought was rational but, the word PARALLEL UNIVERSE itself seems like imagination as no-one has ever seen it and it is unperceivable so, how could you thought that you can prove such a complex thing?" But the answer given by Regal impressed the chairman. As she said "that's what the point sir! No-one has ever seen it thus, they think it's just an imagination but, there is also other possibility that it might exist as none has seen it. What if it really exists? I'm clear sir that EVERY STORY IS POSSIBLE UNTILL IT IS NOT. So, what's wrong in trying to find a way even, it's outcome is negative at least there will be a particular idea of not having it" likewise

She illustrated her ideas. Listening to her the chairman said "Girl! Your thoughts really impressed me. Even the theories stating that the parallel universe is hypothetical and currently having no evidences but, still your words are pleasing me to believe in. Now I'm feeling like what if it really exists! You made me think deep but, still it can't be promoted only based on words. But, really I want to give you a chance to find evidences for it"

Her grey eyes shone and twinkled and happiness started to dance on her face. She immediately accepted the opportunity

 The beautiful red faced girl with grey eyes, escorted by long eye lashes along with celestial nose surrounded by freckles and the perfectly proportioned lips, the blonde hair along her back with a perfectly structured body in a pale coloured skin, wearing a light blue knee length skirt and white canvas shoes, seemed so happy as she finally got an opportunity to prove her fantasy.

It was not just an opportunity to her but it was the moment she was awaiting for. It was such a big thing for a girl who has grown within a science environment reading physics instead of story books, playing with atomic models instead of toys, blasting the smoke with chemical reactions instead of fumes in kitchen, collecting rain water instead of dancing in rain, unlocking theories instead of over thinking......Exploring the world by observing each and every atom.

When it comes to her whereabouts, her home was a big villa with number of facilities and innumerable memories, which was unused when she was left alone. She shut that house and currently living in a single room, which has a universe hidden inside. Her room looked a mess with a lot of things lying on ground. Some spilled on chair and some were leaked from bottles and the bed was set up in a corner as it has used unlikely. The room was filled with a lot of books and grubby things which might look dirty or unclean to others but she never cleaned her room completely as, she never wanted to let any atom out of her room which was only hers. She was really a lover of physics. In her tiny universe, she was not alone.

She was accompanied by her dearest friend SNICKY, a cute white coloured hamster.

Finally she made her mind to clean the room for the analysis of the evidences to prove her dream can be a reality. It completely took a week to set up everything with a classified adjustment. Now the room looked like a room.

She started to read everything related to quantum physics. She grabbed her old books and those tiny encyclopaedias of her childhood which have greatly influenced her in that field.

She never felt bored of what she was doing, as it was not a work for her but her life. She was deeply immersed in her work that she even forgot to eat. But she never uncared Snicky, as it was the only one,

Whom, she loved up to the ends after her father.

Some of her days were spent only under the light of the lamp. Life went on.....

As it took her six weeks to come to a conclusion that not only she believed in parallel universe, but many scientists too gave their theories for parallel universe. And the one, her inspiration and her role model STEPHEN HAWKINGS before his death claimed a theory showing signs to the way of parallel universe.

There, she was called on by the chairman. The chairman asked her whether she had any progress to show to their professors who have been pressurising for giving such an opportunity to a student. She said that she didn't found any evidence still but, she can explain them and had some technical theories. So, the chairman arranged a conference where professors of astrophysics, cosmophysics, quantum physics including MCDougal too attended. She presented her ideas and all were carefully listening to her. But MCDougal doesn't like it. Even though he was good in his profession but he wasn't in his character. He thought that if Regal convinces those members of conference and shows evidences then she might become so popular and she will be the first person to describe such a complex thing. But Regal was not doing all those for popularity but, she had a deep intention behind that. But short minded MCDougal was not able to digest that. So he wontedly interrupted while she was explaining asked her, "you girl! You are going on stating whatever comes to your mind. We don't want your words or assumptions, we want evidences."

Regal desperately said, "Currently I'm too working on it. Still I'm in progress; I need some time to prove this." MCDougal thought it was the exact time low her and started argue, "You can't and you'll never, because no-one in the history have done this. So how could you thought that you can do this only based on your assumptions. Are we looking like fools to you? Even the great scientists never talked about this and you came saying that you can prove this. How silly?" Humiliated Regal busted, "'we are not down to a single unique universe but our findings imply a significant redactor of the multiverse to a much smaller range of possible universe' said Stephen hawking. This makes the theory more predictable and testable. So, what will you say now, was Stephen hawking too making silly statements?"

 There was a minute pause, he seemed to speak, but changed his mind. He was left with nothing to say. Everyone was much impressed with her idea.

But one of them said, "It's okay, it is believable, but how could you find? Or what happens after finding it? And what if you can't find it?"

The chairman boasted, "This is was I wanted to tell you. You all never believed

in such things but now you all gone such deep that you are thinking, what after finding it? This is the magic of this girl, when she can make you from having no interest to think deep, I have full trust on her that surely she will either find a way leading to it or a way which doesn't work. Even, its outcome is negative there will be a certain idea that this way doesn't work." Everyone applauded for 'STELLA REGAL' option less MCDougal too.

2

She drove to home. At the length, she made all their minds that there is a possibility of its existing. But eventually she was stuck in her own mind, what to do next and how to do as she had no evidence, no confirmation she was only left with hypothetical theories, but she didn't lose her hope.

She started to do practical work on her theories. She was completely immersed in her work. She was done with her theoretical work. She finally came to an idea and started to go with her experimental work. She began with a small experiment with prism and did a lot. She all began with a primary work and then she came to an objective of cosmology. She needed some data variables which she didn't had with her but they could be found at MCDougal. She needed them immediately so she drove to MCDougal's home and knocked the door at 1:30am. It was high time that MCDougal has slept but

He was having a drink with his friend who was a cop. On seeing Regal at that time left Dougal speechless. She asked her professor that she needed some things. MCDougal brought the variables from his lab and gave to her without any hesitation.

Regal started to drove home; on her way she was shockingly thinking that why Dougal did gave her those things without any query. She was confused but she had much more things to focus on other than Dougal.

A cosmic ray detection experiment has found particles that could be form a parallel realm that also was born in the big bang. She carried out her experiment using a giant balloon high above where there would be no radio noise to distort its findings.

It completely took six months for her work, to come to an end. She was left with her observations and noted readings. According to her the experiment was done. As she found, evidence and she was so happy that she half way there to her dream of her life.

But her work was undone without experimental analysis. She was just left with a small work to end the experiment. But then she thought about MCDougal as it was being six months that she didn't returned his objectives and she was running out of her food needs. She went to store and bought some food materials and the favourite biscuits of Snicky. In the same store MCDougal too was there. He observed Regal unnoticeably. Then there she came across MCDougal and handed his objectives and thanked him.

Dougal invited her to his home for coffee. She was so astonished but she thought it might be rude if she didn't go. So she went there, MCDougal's behaviour was so   stunning. He introduced Regal to his wife and told that she was his student who was working on a big mission and he was so glad for her. Regal was amazed with his polite behaviour. Later on she wanted to leave and in hurry she forgot her grocery bag but was reminded by her professor. On the way back to her home she was thinking that due to her work, MCDougal changed his mind and started to behave politely with her.

She went home, there she cooked her dinner and fed Snicky his favourite biscuits. She enjoyed her own company and then she began her final step of her work. She started to note down the analytical observation. Insanely her eyes fell on Snicky, who was lying on the ground movement less. She just stopped her work and looked snicky carefully. Snicky appeared so sick that he can't even move. She was scared about what might have happened to her dearest friend. Irrespective of time she took snicky to hospital at midnight. It was raining outside looked like a beginning of storm but she didn't cared. It was lightening and thundering. She went to hospital there snicky was diagnosed and was found to be food poisoned.

The night seemed so dark unless, a big bright thunder hit the ground. It appeared like destroying someone's living. It was completely unable for her to go back to her home in that storm. So she had to spend that night at her friend's home, which was not so far from the hospital.

Next morning she drove to her home. It was very traffic jammed, the police and a big crowd was gathered there. She was surprising got out of her car and saw that..........

She broke down as her complete universe was destroyed. She was never ready for such a thing that might destroy her life and her only dream.

The news was spread all over the city,

'RAIN, STORM BATTER PARTS OF
CALIFORNIA, UPROOT TREES AND
SURRISINGLY DESTROYED A SINGLE HOUSE'

She was left homeless.

3

Her whole work has gone in vain. Years of her hard work, childhood's dream and life's goal was destroyed. After losing her parents in her childhood, it was her only thing which she felt as her everything. She lost that too.

Sighs......

 She had two ways now, either to end up everything and join any job or to start it over again. But she didn't choose any of the two ways. She couldn't end up everything like that and she can't ever join a job just to make her living without any interest. Even though, if she wants to start again it might take her years and she didn't had that much time because next week she had to submit her evidential observation in conference.

She attended the conference only with theoretical hypothesis. She knew that no-one will accept that. She was bugged off. She lost the trust of

conference members and of the chairman too. She
just left the place.

She drove to a public park and sat there, laying her
head on the bench with a stream of thoughts in
her mind.

No-one could predict what was going in her mind but genuinely nothing was running in her mind. The children playing in the park, people walking, talking didn't catch her eyes. She was there, movement less.

There stood someone staring barely at her, looking astonished that how could the girl who used to be always busy with her own mess, came out in a public place. It's really a thing of wonder, but what would have happened?

A loud shout like, "Regal" that person called. Despondent Regal looked here and there but was unable to reach out to the person who called but a pair of curious eyes caught her attention. The person started to walk towards her, wearing a blue jeans accompanying a white jumper t-shirt, carrying some stuff in a polythene bag seemed to have come to enjoy alone but it was a fortunate moment for him to see Regal there. He went to her, silence was shattered eyes started to speak. Those looks weren't unfamiliar. Her eyes spoke volumes and somehow it looked like she had sorrow which she had been bottling up. Finally the silence scattered and the words broke out,"Hey! ADDIE how are you?" she babbled. "So finally you recognized me" he claimed. Although they were childhood friends, separated in high school and met each other after a long time.

The gossip went on. A lot of childhood memories were gathered in their hearts, with elapse of time everything was changed but the bond remained unchanged. They walked the way to their old school bridge, found their childhood spot and sat there. He offered her drink. They enjoyed each other's company.

Staring at the school she said, "Everything was good and life was happy at that time, right?" he re joined saying, "Nothing is as nostalgic as remembering our childhood memories"

"I think I shouldn't have asked this but, you aren't looking completely well has anything happened?" he asked."Nothing is like that, everything is okay." She responded. Unless giving him time to ask something else she countered, "Sorry, I got a rush. I have to leave. We'll meet again." And she left the place in a hurry. He shouted her name but she didn't even look back.

It seemed like she was taken back to her past where, she had everything, her parents, and her friends but, happiness wasn't there anymore. She was only left with those memories. The night went on tears, without falling down.

The next day he found her at the river bank where, she was talking with snicky unwisely. He yelled, "Why didn't you say that your home was destroyed? Why didn't you even thought it necessary to share with me?

"But how did you know about this?" she asked.

"Yesterday I went to your home to return your headscarf that you forgot yesterday in park but not only you your home too wasn't there and then I found what has happened." "Ok so finally you too know what has happened then no worry" she desperately exclaimed.

"So what about your dream now?" he curiously questioned her. Frailty expressed "Maybe my dream is really just an imagination so destiny too doesn't wanted to happen"

Astonishingly he asked "So are you giving up on it? it's not the destiny doesn't wanted but those are the people who don't want to see you achieving your goals"

"What are you talking" She dazed.

 "yes you don't lost your home and your work due to any natural calamity or storm it is a well planned game, you are trapped in it." he told

 "I don't believe in it. why would someone destroy my house and my living what would I have done to them?"

"I know you won't believe it I am not like you to speak without any proof yesterday I myself have seen a cop near your home he was not on his duty but he was doing something against law I heard him talking on his mobile about the money he was asking someone for destroying your home."

4

"Is this true?" she stunningly asked

"Trust me, we can find that person only if you believe in me" he gave her a hope

"But who was that cop" she queried

"I too don't know but if we follow him we can find that person who is behind all this"

" But how can we find that cop in this huge city?"

"I have a plan" he giggled in her ears

Next morning Regal without hesitation drove to chairman office everyone was surprised to see her there after such a big tragedy. she directly entered his cabin and they both had a good talk everyone seemed so curious that what talk might be going there after sometime she left the place and she entered the NASA headquarters there she met her old friend to talked for a while and left to her home.

The day has passed. She went to her new rented home. She cooked some food and enjoyed her dinner with snicky in her balcony it appeared like someone was trying to enter her home she thought it might be her friend Addie so she gave a loud shout "come up Addie! Let's have dinner"

But fractionally, Addie was on the street road waving his hand to her.

"If he is still on the street road then who was that trying to enter the home?" she suspiciously questioned herself. she ran down to catch that person. On seeing her, that person started to run. Addie seen the person running from Regal's house and he chased him but he couldn't catch. However, their plan worked because they at least has known that someone is spying. The person who came today then he will surely try to come next day too.

Three days gone. None seemed suspicious. Regal was desperately drown into thinking that it all started when she took snicky to hospital she was talking to herself that if she hadn't went to hospital that night then the person behind all this, would have killed her too. Then, entered Addie stating, "Why the hell would he kill you? If he wanted to kill you he might have done it simply but things are so complex here"

Regal gravely asked, "what would they are trying to take away from me?"

 He doubtlessly said, "It's all about your work. They destroyed your home not to kill you but to kill your dream and hope. see, if wanted to kill you they wouldn't have taken this much of time but everything was ok until you gave up on your work but according to our plan when you went to chairman office they thought that you are planning something. so they started to spy you again because they don't know that you went to chairman to just talk about a home for rental in headquarters"

 They both started to walk on the streets talking about their plant and there, they came across a man and he gestured Regal to see that men on seeing that man Regal wished him that how he was?

Addie was surprised and asked that whether she knew that person she said that she was a cop and a good friend of his professor and three MCDougal.

"Then no doubt the person behind all this mess is someone who closely knows you" he prompted

"What?"

"Yes, because the Cop who is the person whom I have seen that night at your home"

When they looked back the cop hesitantly started to run. They confirmed that he had a hand in this and finally they caught him and took to her house although that cop was corrupted he had to obey his blunder. Ultimately he reveals the truth that it was all done by MCDougal.

She shattered down.

The Cop told, "Yes it is he who changed the biscuits of your pet with poisonous biscuits in your grocery bag when, he invited you for coffee. It was well planned that when you take your pet to hospital your work analysis should be theft and to destroy your home. It was not a thunder but a blast arranged by an artificial lightning that day weather too supported us and everyone thought it was a thunder but, when we entered your home for your analysis it wasn't there so we just destroyed your home. MCDougal thought now you don't have anyone evidence but when you again went to meet chairman we thought that you still have something and you were trying to start something new. So, we sent a person to spy you but this boy, your friend destroyed our plan" he claimed pointing towards Addie

She was exhausted.

"Let's go to MCDougal" he declared.

"I didn't even want to see his face let the law take action against this" she awfully teared and ran into her room

The Cop, MCDougal and the persons who were involved in that were arrested.

5

She was drowned in the ocean of sorrow she was not in a condition to listen anyone that time but she don't know what why how.....

 Literally she knew nothing

He too didn't know what to do.

Days went on.

 He didn't want her to lose hope although, she was his childhood crush, and how could he leave her at such hard times.

He went to her home and said her to pack her bags as he wanted her to take for a wonderful trip, but as usually she didn't wanted to come.

But this time he forced her by giving a hope he asked "what is your name?" irritably she said "Are you mad? Don't you know my name?"

"You just tell me what it is" he repeated again

 "It's Regal!" she told

"your full name?" again he asked

"Stella Regal" she shouted

"That's what I wanted to let you know"

 "What, my name? Are you serious? Stop your silly talks" she yelled

 "Just come with me I want to show you something"

He took her in his car and drove long.

California to San Francisco it was a pleasant road trip. She too seemed to calm her mind. From San Francisco they boarded. She thought that he might want to comfort her with the holiday trip but she didn't know what he had known about her.

The flight took off.

After a mere journey of five hours they landed in Hawaii.

He took her to some Adventurous places and tried to make her feel better but it doesn't work. He waited till the Dawn.

The sun had been set down the darkness spread over the sky. Nevertheless, it was Hawaiian night how wouldn't be those Nights interesting.

She was tired of the journey but still he took her to the most beautiful and the world's premier astronomical destination the MAUNAKEA summit on the big Island perhaps, the most famous stargazing spot in Hawaii.

The night sky inspired such awe and capturing that sense of awe has been found to turn them into better.

He shouted "Stella Regal"

She naively looked towards him but he was pointing towards the Sky.

She artlessly looked towards the sky.

"There Stella Regal" he said "your name itself came from this universe and Stella Regal meant the name of this stars" he pointed.

That hit her mind.

She restated his words saying "Regal is not a star" said "it's an Orion, a group of stars in the sky that looks like a hunter with the line of three bright starts for a belt but Stella mean star" she claimed.

"This is what I wanted to make you feel. You are not a useless thing in this world but you are a part of this universe so how could you lose your hope and your dream of mirror world.

I have seen you from my childhood that how excited you used to be when your dad used to tell about parallel universe you repeat it Mirror world"

His words were flowing in background, she was unconsciously hearing him she was immersed in gazing that night sky that eased her mind and rejuvenated her spirit it made her more compassionate towards herself. She found herself searching for peace, calm and the sense of purpose during that period of immense chaos. She was not alone she was with entire universe.

6

"But how do you know all this? I don't think you have this much of knowledge about astronomy and who told you about my name?"

"Your father"

"What, But When?"

"Just a week back"

"Oh! You again started your nonsense"

"no, I'm serious about it," he gave a diary to her

"It's my dad's diary! But where did you found this?"

"On that day when I went to your destroyed house, found this but, I founded half burnt"

She was looking at the diary like it was her only left treasure

"I know after your mother's death your father was everything but I didn't know how your father death was happened at the time I wasn't with you as we were separated in our Secondary School" he affirmed.

"Yes, my dad was everything. You know, my dream to prove parallel universe existence is not just a goal but it's my only hope.

 After my mother's death, whenever I asked about my mother my dad used to tell me that I can meet her in mirror world.

During that innocent childhood that was my fantasy to meet my mother in mirror world but, as I grew up I realized that my father was just trying to give me a temporary satisfaction.

But I was very happy with my father. He was my complete universe and I was this ultimate world. Everything was happy. He never made me feel that incompleteness of my mother. And he gave me everything.

It's very tiny if I described him as the world's best father but, he was my superhero.

But this destiny can't digest happy faces.

It was my birthday; he gifted me a friend that was Snicky. We celebrated it simply as he had to leave for his mission. I was handed over to my aunt Claire until my dad completes his mission. I think you have heard about 'space shuttle Challenger disaster'

It was launched on 28th of January from Florida that was the 10th mission with the aim of deploying, tracking and data relay satellite and to observe Halley's Comet

Challenger was at that time the most flown Orbiter in NASA's fleet setting numerous records.

My father was an astronaut so, I can't say he left to his mission on my birthday but that Mission was earlier postponed from seven days. Seven crew members were primed for that mission and my father was one of them.

I and Aunt Claire were unable to reach Florida, because on the night before the final launch day Central Florida was swept by a severe cold wave.

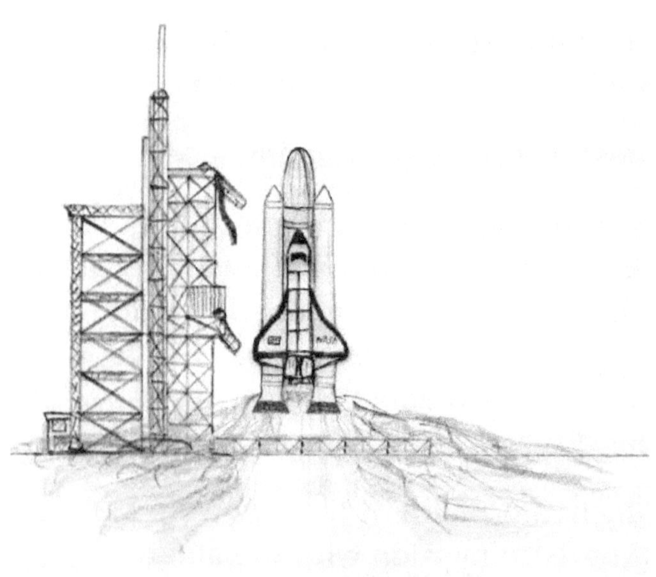

All appeared to be normal on the morning of launch. When, thousands of people on the ground and millions of people were watching

Live including us witnessed a wrenching tragedy, an explosion just 73 seconds after liftoff.

Lives of 7 people and thousands of their family members were demolished.

The anxiety between those 73 seconds turned to sorrow of a lot of people. And that was the unimaginable and unforgettable incident in my life. I was not even fortunate for my father's cremation.

I was left with nothing. Being a 16 year old girl I was unable to digest that. My Night sleeps were drained, my mornings for exhausted I was completely destroyed. I had a million reasons to end my life at that situation but, there came a hope in my life. I remembered my Father's words that I could meet him in mirror world. So I started to know about it. I finally came to know that there was a possibility of parallel universe. I started to research about it and I found a lead but, that was destroyed. This was the ultimate way to meet my parents. Whatever I have done it's all for my father and this is the reason why I am mad about mirror world" she described her past.

7

Listening to her past his eyes were filled, start for drowning in those tears. The whole night went in their gossip.

The next morning he told her to pack the bags and to get ready for another surprising place.

She was amazed of what might be going in his mind.

They travelled to Norway.

That night he introduced her to the prettiest envisaging place to capture the dark Sky with Aurora Borealis, filled with vibrant colours glitter and light up the night sky in a display of natural beauty. She was bewildered on seeing such a magical Sky.

He uttered, "no 3 dimensions can halt to see this impressive view" he exclaimed.

"Dimensions!" she nodded.

He looked towards her abruptly.

She immensely said, "fourth dimension!"

"What is that?" he asked

"Just now you told no three dimensions could stop to see this view" she repeated his words.

"Yes I did" he said

"But what about fourth dimension?" her eyes filled with fascination

"But what is the fourth dimension?" he stupefied.

"TIME" she whizzed.

"But why are you talking about it now?" he questioned

She hopefully told," I think my last work was not really an end of my dream we can find a way to it through this fourth dimension"

"Are you serious?"

"Yes, we have a possibility!" she admired.

Ideas were wandering in her mind. Her father once uses this word fourth dimension to inspire her but now she was arranging up her plan based with fourth dimension. This time she seemed unpredictable.

8

She was back to her work. By this time she had no back pullers except her own thoughts.

He asked her what she was working for. She replied," it may seem odd to you, but it was just before I could follow up the new found clue in what was manifesting the proper way"

"I didn't even get a bit" he exclaimed.

"A Time Traveller machine"

His Expression left no words to explain.

"Trust the process" she deduced.

She started her work. It went on evenly without any hesitation. Time went on, days were gone, and months were running. Everything looked irony, the glitter metallic framework, scarcely larger than a small clock, which was very delicately made. There was Ivory in it, and some transparent crystalline substances.

Unless that the small octagonal tables that were scattered about the room and set in front of the Fire, with two legs on the hearthrug. On this table she placed the mechanism. Then she Drew up a chair and sat down. The only other object on the table was a small shaded lamp, the bright light of with fell upon the model.

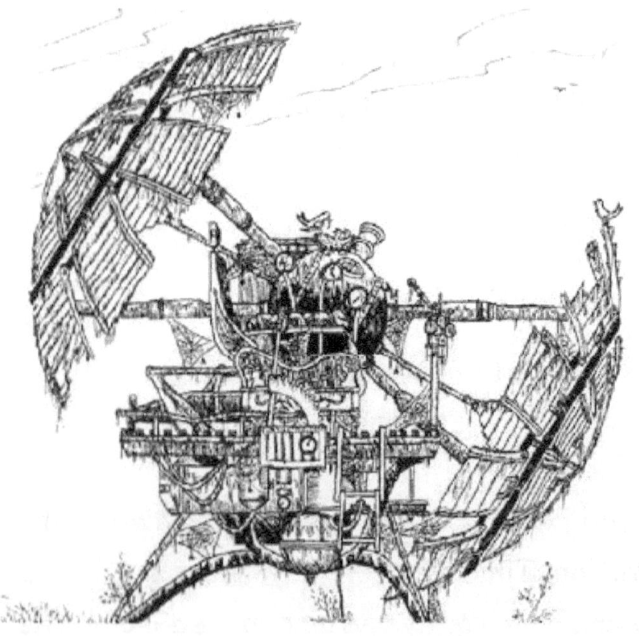

Finally life was breathed into her imagination.

She was immensely Happified.

"Addie! Look at this my dream came true, I can't even believe this"

She shared her happiness with him. He never left her side in sorrow or in her rejoice too. Things seemed jovial but the real trouble was unidentified.

"Does this really work?" he asked.

"Obviously yes, and now it's the time I must do this"

"But I don't think this is really a good option"

"What happened? Why are you talking like that?" she boasted

Their argument was going on whether to travel in that or not

"Do you doubt my invention?" she proclaimed

"No, not at all, but I am scared about you. I don't want to lose you"

"Nothing will happen let me try this and you just operate it" she instructed.

She switched it on. He started to operate it. That model was chokingly started with a low voice and seemed so incredible. He was so scared and she was so excited.

Wearing an advanced tech suit in front of Quantum tunnel, the time was set for the date where she could meet her parents. She was just to step in it but unimaginably Snicky went in with a forcible run. That machine got locked with the entry of it. Snicky was off tracked into the past. Being a small creature and that too, a pet it

doesn't even know about its return,

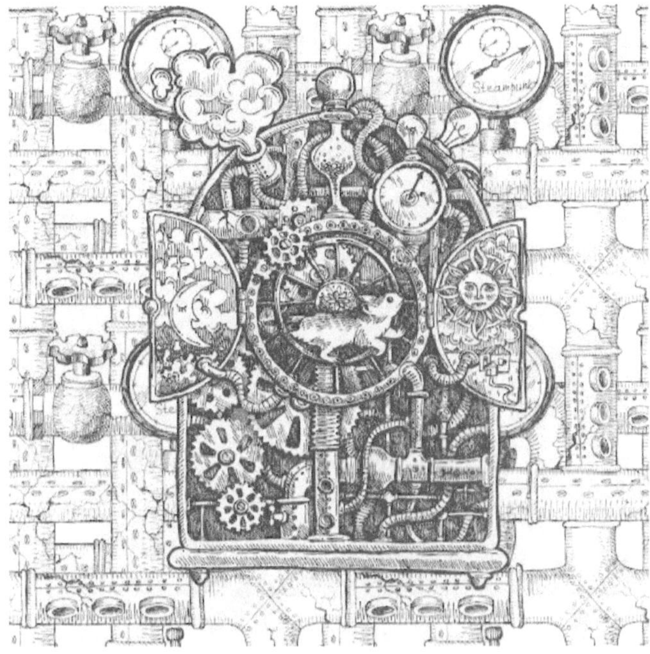

it was endured in a lost city.

 She was left with suffocation of what has happened. She was not able to understand how that little creature could come back. She without delaying a second started to reset her invention.

"Where has it gone?" he asked

"To that place where I supposed to go"

"How could it come back? as it doesn't know anything"

"I too don't know, he didn't even had any Time Space GPS"

"Is there any other way to get him back?"

"I reset this, it may take 24 hours if this works properly then our snicky will be back in 24 hours"

"Let's hope for the best" He said.

9

That night she didn't sleep well. Probably her health was a little disordered. She was oppressed with perplexity and doubt. Once or twice she had a feeling of intense fear for which she could perceive no definite reason. She remembered that creepy noiseless, great hall where the little snicky used to sleep in the moonlight.

The morning Sun began to rise her eyes were hunting the whole house that some miracle could happen. Every second seemed like a year for her to spend. Her eyes were on clock. It was been more than 14 hours.

"10 Hours more" she uplifted her heart.

Addie brought some food but it was so hard for the throat to swallow anything. Time was really a healer and the killer she felt that.

It was so auspicious it had been more than 24 hours and nothing seemed to work out. She was lying on the carpet with the hearth behind and a million thoughts in her mind. She lost her hope and snicky too.

She had gone astray.

She screamed out loudly that she was a failure. She cried out loud and louder. She blamed herself that her theories were nonsense and so stupid. She Low hearted herself. She not just lost her interest in parallel Universe but she lost herself too.

She screamed, screeched and bawled but she can't get back anyone neither her loved ones nor she could go to them.

She fell ill and gone into sleep.

10

The darkness was spread in her heart and in the sky too. That was the moment when each and every Atom was Hushed.

It sounded like an alarm but it isn't. She quietly came conscious; it looked like something was brightly shining. She ran into the hall. Those were the lights radiating from her invented machine; a hope got lit with those light. The Machine slowly started to work with slight chocking noises.

The door got open, but snicky wasn't there. She was startled that what might happen.

Without taking a second thought she stepped in. The machine again got locked with her entry. She was not able to understand what was happening but door opened. She stepped out, that was the same place where she stepped in but this time that place was unfamiliar. She went out, everything was normal but nothing seemed ok. Everything was similar to her place but the scenario was different in the same town. She ran in those streets. She went to her old destroyed house, but that wasn't destroyed. That was as it was without any change. She was confused that whether she entered Past or stepped in a parallel universe. If that was past, new buildings shouldn't be there but that was exact to her reality, except the difference of her destroyed house.

She was dazzlingly looking at that place when something made her eyes to move, something ran down on her feet. She looked down, that was snicky. Her face lighted up with happiness. She felt like life was back again to her body. Snicky started to run towards the lake. She too ran behind it.

There she found love. She found hand to hold under shoulder to lay her head on. She found her superhero and the most beautiful person she ever met. She found her parents.

Joy scattered everywhere, there were colours of happiness in the sky, and the place was enlightened with the rays of fortune.

"Look, where I have come, heavens are right here, sun, moon, everything all here been waiting for ages" she uttered herself.

The sky bowed down to the will of that little girl's hope.

Everything was happy.....until she woke up.

THE END

Do you believe in parallel universe?

www.ingramcontent.com/pod-product-compliance
Lightning Source LLC
Chambersburg PA
CBHW031241130726
47988CB00008B/3174